A BANK STREET MUSEUM BOOK

OCEANARIUM

By Joanne Oppenheim • Illustrated by Alán Gutierrez

With an introduction by Ellie Fries and Merryl Kafka, Science Consultants

A Byron Preiss Book

BANTAM BOOKS
NEW YORK • TORONTO • LONDON • SYDNEY • AUCKLAND

To Kate, Allie, Emmy,
Adam, and Matthew
—J.O.

OCEANARIUM

A Bantam Book / March 1994

Series graphic design by Alex Jay/Studio J
Senior Editor: Sarah Feldman
Assistant Editor: Kathy Huck
Special thanks to Betsy Gould, Hope Innelli,
James A. Levine, and Howard Zimmerman.

Library of Congress Cataloging-in-Publication Data

Oppenheim, Joanne.
Oceanarium/by Joanne Oppenheim;
illustrated by Alan Gutierrez;
with an introduction by Ellen Fries
and Merryl Kafka, science consultants.
p.   cm.—(A Bank Street museum book)
"A Byron Preiss book."
Includes index.
ISBN 0-553-09361-4—ISBN 0-553-37128-2
1. Marine fauna—Juvenile literature.   2. Marine aquariums,
Public—Juvenile literature.   I. Gutierrez, Alan.   II. Title.
III. Series.
QL122.2.067 1994
591.92—dc20
93-3157
CIP
AC

Published simultaneously in the United States and Canada

PRINTED IN THE UNITED STATES OF AMERICA

0 9 8 7 6 5 4 3 2 1

Introduction

Beneath the waves of the beautiful blue sea lies a world filled with many fantastic plants and animals.

As you explore the ocean life described in the pages of this book, you will make many new discoveries. Remember, however, that the marine environment is a fragile ecosystem delicately balanced to support all the wonderful life forms that call it home.

Let us pledge to keep our oceans clean and healthy so they will always be safe, productive habitats for all the plants and animals from anemones to zebrafish. Join the "wave" for conservation and share your enthusiasm for the environment with your friends and family.

Ellie Fries,
Director of Education
Merryl Kafka,
Assistant Director
of Education
New York Aquarium

Welcome to the Oceanarium. You are about to dip into the underwater world of the sea. Our specially constructed elevator will give you a close-up view of some of the amazing animals and plants that live in the world's oceans.

TABLE OF CONTENTS

BRIEFING ROOM
PAGES 6–11

TIDAL WATERS
PAGES 12–13

COASTAL WATERS
PAGES 14–17

THE CORAL REEF
PAGES 18–21

FLATFISH
PAGES 22–23

THE OPEN SEA
PAGES 24–25

SCHOOLS OF FISH
PAGES 26–29

THE DEEP SEA
PAGES 30–33

SHARK TANK
PAGES 34–39

SKATES AND RAYS
PAGES 40–41

SEA MAMMALS
PAGES 42–45

SAVE OUR SEAS!
PAGES 46–47

INDEX
PAGE 48

BRIEFING ROOM

There are about twenty-four thousand species of fish in the ocean. Where they live usually depends on the temperature of the water. Most fish cannot survive outside their own environment. Many fish can live only in warm tropical waters; others can live only in temperate waters, which are neither very warm nor very cold. Still others live their entire lives in the icy waters of the Arctic and Antarctic oceans.

Before we begin our dive, take a few moments to study these charts. They will help you to understand what you are about to see.

Arctic Ocean   POLAR

North America   TEMPERATE

Pacific Ocean   TROPICAL

EQUATOR   South America   TROPICAL
Atlantic Ocean

TEMPERATE

Antarctica   POLAR

Continents and Oceans of the World

What Makes a Fish a Fish?
Fish come in many shapes, colors, and sizes. There are four things that are true about all fish:
• They have backbones.
• They have gills for breathing oxygen underwater.
• They have fins for balance and/or movement.
• They are cold-blooded (their body temperature is about the same as the temperature of the water in which they live).

ANATOMY OF A FISH

All fish are vertebrates, which means they have backbones. Some fish, such as sharks and rays, have skeletons made of cartilage, which is softer than bone. Others have skeletons made of both bone and cartilage. But the vast majority of fish have skeletons made only of bone; they are called modern bony fish.

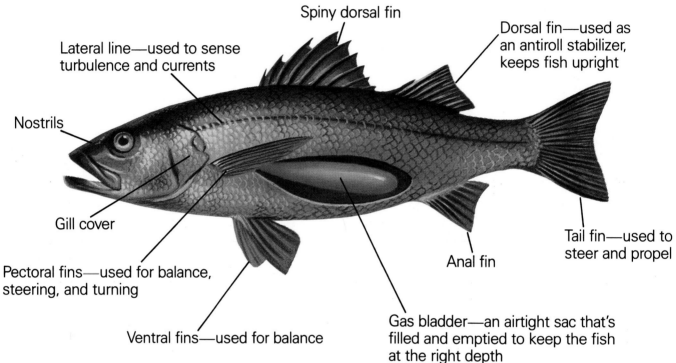

Spiny dorsal fin

Dorsal fin—used as an antiroll stabilizer, keeps fish upright

Lateral line—used to sense turbulence and currents

Nostrils

Gill cover

Tail fin—used to steer and propel

Anal fin

Pectoral fins—used for balance, steering, and turning

Ventral fins—used for balance

Gas bladder—an airtight sac that's filled and emptied to keep the fish at the right depth

Tuna

Bowfin

The shape, size, and location of the fins affect a fish's speed. Fish with deeply forked, crescent-shaped tails are generally fast swimmers. Fish with squared or rounded tails are often slow swimmers. Which of these fish is the faster swimmer?

How do fish breathe?

Like all other animals, fish need oxygen to breathe. Fish get their oxygen from the water, which is a compound of hydrogen and oxygen. First the water goes into their mouths. It passes through their gills and then out through openings in the sides of their heads, taking in oxygen from the water and removing carbon dioxide. This is what you do when you breathe air—you take in oxygen and breathe out carbon dioxide. Some ocean-dwelling creatures are mammals. They have lungs and must come up to the surface for air.

One of these creatures does not have gills. Which do you think it is? If you said whale, you're right! A whale is a mammal and has lungs. It must come to the surface for air.

Haddock

Shark

Whale

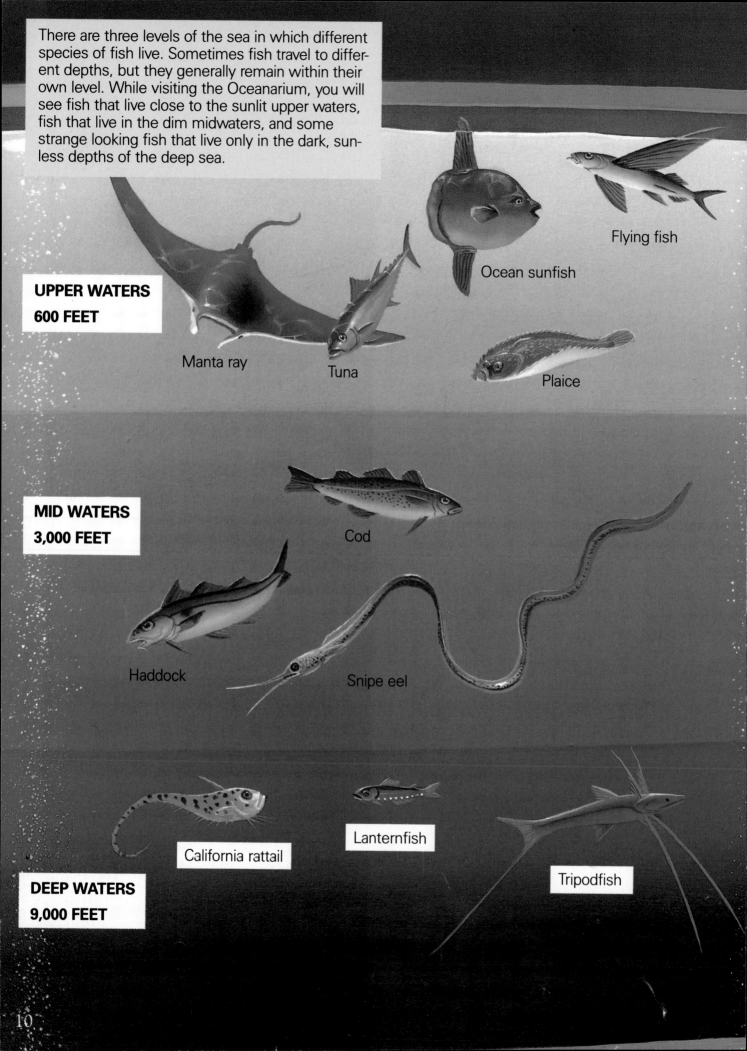

There are three levels of the sea in which different species of fish live. Sometimes fish travel to different depths, but they generally remain within their own level. While visiting the Oceanarium, you will see fish that live close to the sunlit upper waters, fish that live in the dim midwaters, and some strange looking fish that live only in the dark, sunless depths of the deep sea.

UPPER WATERS
600 FEET

Flying fish

Ocean sunfish

Manta ray

Tuna

Plaice

MID WATERS
3,000 FEET

Cod

Haddock

Snipe eel

DEEP WATERS
9,000 FEET

California rattail

Lanternfish

Tripodfish

11

TIDAL WATERS

As we enter the sea, the pounding tide rushes over the shore. Here, anchored on rocks, clinging to underwater forests of seaweed, or riding on waves, an astounding variety of young fish and invertebrates find a safe haven. Many will move to deeper waters when they grow up.

In the intertidal zone, where the tides flow in and out, there are creatures that have adapted to living without water for short periods of time. Many of the fish found in such an environment are slow-moving and tend to live in one place.

What are invertebrates?

They are animals without backbones, like crabs, shrimp, and jellyfish.

Longhorn sculpin

Porcupine fish

Pipefish

Shanny

Blenny

Sea robin

Crab

Worm

Jellyfish

Shrimp

Barnacle

12

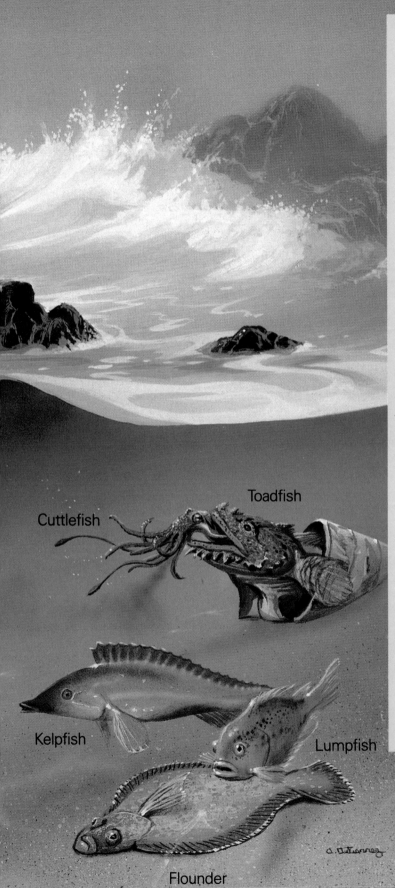

Toadfish

Cuttlefish

Kelpfish

Lumpfish

Flounder

Blennies are found from the tropics to the polar waters. Some have scales, while others do not. Blennies are commonly found in tidal pools.
Length: 2–5 inches

Kelpfish have mottled skin that provides camouflage to hide them as they swim among the tall, swaying kelp beds.
Length: 4–8 inches

Longhorn sculpins have spiny fins and a sharp spine on their armored head. Their blotchy color helps these bottom dwellers hide.
Length: 1 foot

Lumpfish can be found in shallow and deep waters. Their skin looks like the pebbly sea bed, and they have sucker discs like sea snails. Males guard eggs that are laid in sponge clusters.
Length: 20 inches

Pipefish have a long, snoutlike mouth, like a sea horse's mouth. The males carry their young in a breeding pouch until they hatch.
Length: 4–12 inches

Porcupine fish are found in shallow waters. They can inflate their spiny body for protection against predators.
Length: 3 feet

Sea snails are not really snails but tadpole-shaped fish. They have sucker discs on their underside so they can cling to rocks.
Length: 4–6 inches

Shannies have no scales. They can change color to blend with their background and frequently end up in tidal pools at low tide. They hide under rocks and empty shells. Males guard the eggs.
Length: 6 inches

COASTAL WATERS

Here are some of the many fish that live in the coastal waters just off each continent. Some of these fish never swim very far from shore. Others are more far-ranging and travel between tropical and temperate waters, from shallow to deeper waters, or from coastal waters to open seas to find the right temperature, food, or mate.

Mojarra

Menhaden

Atlantic wolffish

Crustaceans

Crustaceans are hard-shelled creatures such as lobsters, shrimp, crabs, or barnacles.

Mollusks are creatures with soft bodies that are all or partly enclosed by shells such as snails, clams, oysters, squid, and octopi.

Atlantic cod have a distinctive snout, a barbel on their chin, and three dorsal fins. Some go south in winter, while others move to deeper waters.
Length: 3 feet

Atlantic wolffish are loners. They use their large, tusklike teeth to feed on mollusks and crustaceans.
Length: 5 feet

Bonefish live in grassy shallow water and feed on mollusks and crustaceans. Bottom feeders, their mouth opens downward.
Length: 3 feet

Menhaden young feed and grow in bays and inlets. Older fish live in open waters. They travel in large schools, swimming close to the surface.
Length: 10 inches

Mojarras are found on both the Atlantic and the Pacific coasts. They can extend their mouth into a long tube when feeding on animals and plants.
Length: 1–12 inches

Sea catfish spend the summer in coastal bays and migrate to deeper water in winter. They have long, trailing pectoral and dorsal fins and barbels on their jaws. The males carry fertilized eggs and hatched young in their mouth for approximately two months (they do not eat during that time!).
Length: 1 foot

Tarpon are silver fish with a very long dorsal fin and large scales that can be up to an inch wide. They travel to shallow waters and even up rivers in pursuit of smaller fish.
Length: 4–8 feet

MORE COASTAL WATER FISH

North American
striped bass

Tripletail

Pigfish

Common jack

Butterfish

Haddock

Butterfish live in sandy bottom water close to shore. They are schooling fish of subtropical and tropical seas.
Length: 6–9 inches

Common jacks live in small schools in coastal waters. They have a deeply forked tail and prefer warm waters.
Length: 2 feet

Haddock are sleeker and smaller relatives of cod. They live in deeper waters (60–600 feet) and are bottom feeders that eat crustaceans, worms, and shellfish.
Length: 2 feet

Needlefish feed on small fish in warm surface waters. They have a long body and a long, toothy jaw.
Length: 12–20 inches

North American striped bass have horizontal stripes, which distinguish them from European sea bass. They like rough waters, where they can pursue schools of mackerel and herring. A big bass can gulp down a whole mackerel. Bass hunt in large schools, but some adults are loners.
Length: Up to 5 feet

Pigfish live around rocks and docks, and feed on whatever animals they find there.
Length: 14 inches

Tripletails have large dorsal and anal fins and look as if they have three tails. They swim on their side or float with their head down. They are found only in warm waters.
Length: 3 feet

THE CORAL REEF

You are now in the warm waters of the coral reef. Some of the most colorful and beautiful fish live here in the tropical waters of the Pacific and Indian Oceans and around the Caribbean islands of the West Indies. Here, near the equator, where the sun heats the water, the sea teems with an amazing variety of plants and creatures that depend on each other.

Most corals grow where the water temperature is at least seventy degrees Fahrenheit.

There are more than a million polyps in a section of living coral about the size of a small chest of drawers!

Here on the coral reef, many things that look like plants are really sea animals. The sea anemone, the sea fan, sea whip, sea plum, and sea cucumber are just a few of them.

Sergeant-major

Sea whip

Parrot fish

Spotted goatfish

A coral reef is formed by billions of tiny cylinder-shaped animals called coral polyps. They feed on plankton, which are tiny plants and animals drifting in the ocean. When a polyp dies, its skeleton is left to become part of the reef. Then new polyps grow on top of the old ones.

Barracudas are swift, sleek, ferocious predators known as "tigers of the sea." They have both long, fang-shaped teeth and shorter, daggerlike teeth to rip and tear their prey apart.
Length: 5–10 feet

Clown butterfly fish have a large "false eye" spot. The spot confuses predators, who cannot tell the tail end from the front end of the fish.
Length: 6–8 inches

Clown fish are colorful fish that have a mutualistic relationship with the sea anemone. This means they take care of each other. They lure other fish into the poisonous tentacles of the sea anemone, and then eat what the sea anemone leaves.
Length: 1–3 inches

Parrot fish have heavy teeth in their throat as well as in their mouth for eating crushed coral. They secrete a cover of mucus to protect themselves from predators like sharks and barracudas while they sleep.
Length: 3 feet

Sergeant-majors are named for the black stripes on their back. Males are extremely aggressive and guard the eggs until they hatch—they will even chase female parents away.
Length: 6 inches

Spotted goatfish can change color rapidly. They have long chin barbels that can be raised and lowered to search for small animals on the sea bed.
Length: 10 inches

An octopus is not a fish; it is a mollusk like a clam or a snail, but it has no shell. Octopi are predators that live in dark holes and caves of coral. They travel on a jet of water they expel by contracting their muscles. They can also crawl with their eight tentacles.

Branching coral

Clown butterfly fish

Sea anemone

Clown fish

Octopus

MORE FISH OF THE CORAL REEF

To escape from hungry predators, fish of the coral reef have different ways of protecting themselves. Some can change color. Others have poisonous spines. Still others are so flat and fast they can escape into places that large fish cannot enter. Some hide by day and feed by night. Others dart among the treelike branches of the reef or burrow in dark limestone caves.

Ocean triggerfish

Queen angelfish

Stonefish

Moray eel

Cleaner wrasses have thick lips; large, strong teeth; and a distinctive stripe. Large predators like the grouper and squirrelfish allow cleaner wrasses to enter their mouths and gills to clean off parasites.
Length: 6 inches

Lionfish have long pectoral fins that spread like a fan. A high dorsal fin with sharp, venomous spines is used for defense against predators.
Length: 8 inches

Moray eels are often called "rattlesnakes of the sea." They have strong, V-shaped jaws with sharp teeth. They hide in rocky holes and snap at intruders. Shrimp cling to their head and eat parasites on their skin.
Length: 3–10 feet

Nassau groupers can change their appearance with spots, stripes, and patches of color. They are predators that gulp down small fish.
Length: 3–5 feet

Ocean triggerfish have a dorsal fin with three sharp spines that rise if they are disturbed. Each fin drops down only when the one next to it is squeezed—like a trigger.
Length: 2 feet

Queen angelfish have a compressed body that enables them to slip between the nooks and crannies of the reef and escape large predators. Their long, sharp spine at the lower edge of the gill cover may be venomous.
Length: 2 feet

Stonefish are deadly. They hide among stones in shallow water; on their back and sides, they have venomous spines which are raised when an enemy approaches.
Length: 10–15 inches

Lionfish

Cleaner wrasse

Sea fan

Pipe coral

Nassau grouper

Sea cucumber

FLATFISH

Most fish have torpedo-shaped bodies, but there are also about six hundred species of flatfish. The majority of flatfish live along the coastal shelves, and all are bottom dwellers. Their flat bodies help to conceal them from predators, and most flatfish can change color to blend in with the sea bed where they lie.

Plaice

Flounder

Halibut

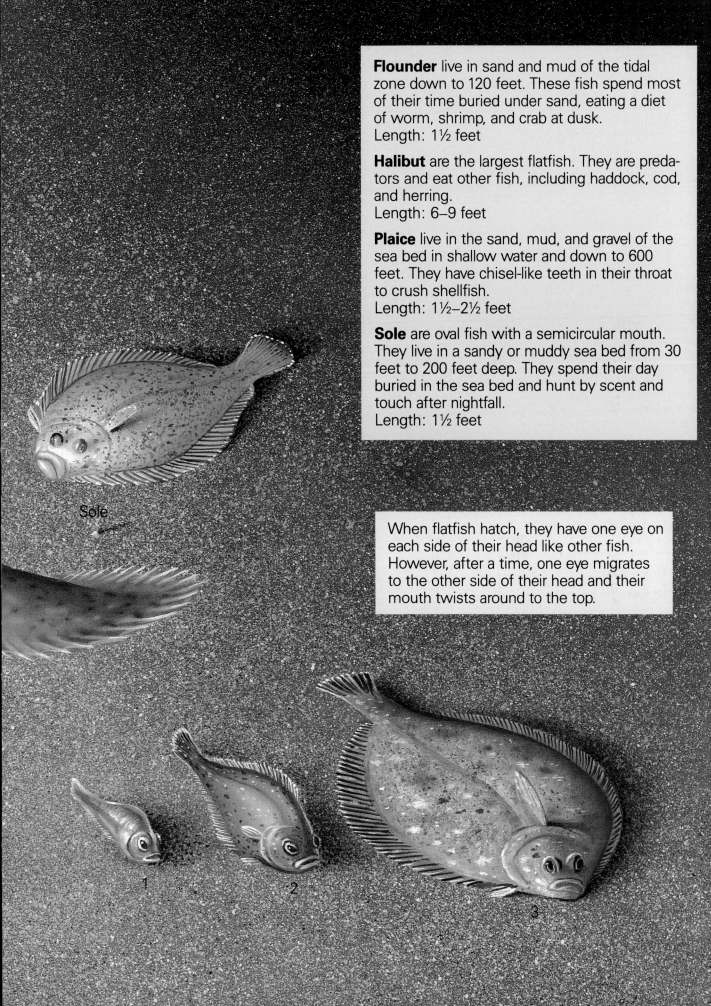

Flounder live in sand and mud of the tidal zone down to 120 feet. These fish spend most of their time buried under sand, eating a diet of worm, shrimp, and crab at dusk.
Length: 1½ feet

Halibut are the largest flatfish. They are predators and eat other fish, including haddock, cod, and herring.
Length: 6–9 feet

Plaice live in the sand, mud, and gravel of the sea bed in shallow water and down to 600 feet. They have chisel-like teeth in their throat to crush shellfish.
Length: 1½–2½ feet

Sole are oval fish with a semicircular mouth. They live in a sandy or muddy sea bed from 30 feet to 200 feet deep. They spend their day buried in the sea bed and hunt by scent and touch after nightfall.
Length: 1½ feet

When flatfish hatch, they have one eye on each side of their head like other fish. However, after a time, one eye migrates to the other side of their head and their mouth twists around to the top.

Sole

1

2

3

THE OPEN SEA

Now we have left the coastal waters and entered the vast expanse of the open sea, where some of the largest and swiftest fish live. Generally, these fish live far from shore and swim in surface water. They pursue huge schools of smaller fish that migrate each year from the tropics to near polar waters.

Flying fish

Ocean sunfish

Sailfish

Dolphin fish

Blue marlin are found in tropic and temperate waters. They have a round, pointed beak, but are smaller than swordfish.
Length: 10–14 feet

Dolphin fish are very fast swimmers. They leap from the water when they are chasing smaller fish or being chased by larger predators. These beautiful multicolored fish live chiefly in the tropics, but migrate north in the summer.
Length: 5–6 feet

Flying fish have winglike fins that allow them to glide over the water. They gather speed underwater and then break the surface when pursued by dolphin fish.
Length: 1½ feet

Ocean sunfish are not related to the sunfish found in fresh water. Sometimes called headfish, these ocean dwellers have no tail. They are slow movers that travel in surface waters carried by the currents. They feed on slow-moving jellyfish and other small invertebrates.
Length: 6 feet

Sailfish have a high and wide dorsal fin, which looks like a sail. They have a rounded, pointed beak. They are often seen in schools pursuing mackerel, menhaden, and other small fish.
Length: 10 feet

Squids are mollusks, not fish. They move by jet propulsion, achieved by the force of the water pushed out of their torpedo-shaped body. Among the fastest-moving creatures, they swim backward into a school of fish and grab with their tentacles.
Length: 10 inches

Swordfish can swim as fast as 60 miles per hour. They live in tropic and warm temperate waters, and may venture into colder waters in the summer. Their beaklike sword is used to kill prey. They follow schools of migrating herring, sardines, and mackerel.
Length: 10–16 feet

SCHOOLS OF FISH

Many predators, such as sharks, are loners. They hunt for their prey alone and seek the companionship of others only when they mate.

Other fish live in groups called schools. There are a great many schooling fish, and each school has a different number of members. A school of herring may have millions of members, while a school of tuna may have fewer than two dozen fish. Interestingly, in any school, all the fish are pretty much the same size, since adult fish do not swim with their young.

Some fish live their entire lives with the same school. Others stay together for just a short time after they hatch. Swimming in great numbers provides some defense against predators. When threatened, a school of fish may form a tight group that can frighten a predator. The members of a school may break formation to feed at night, and then join together when day breaks.

Shark

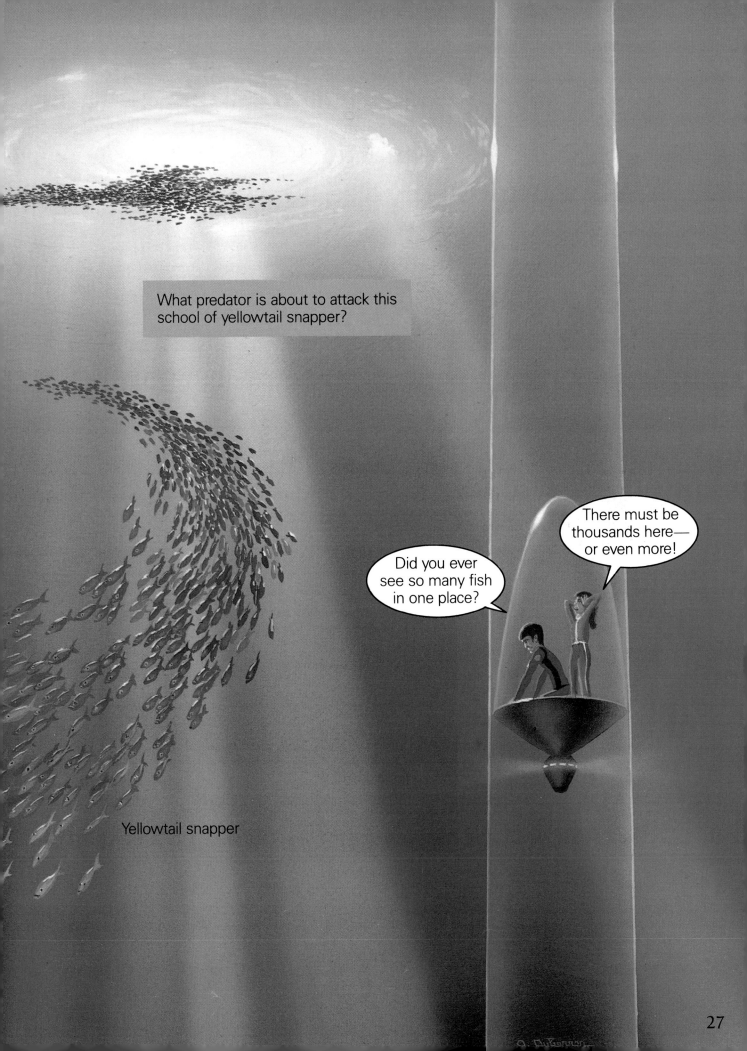

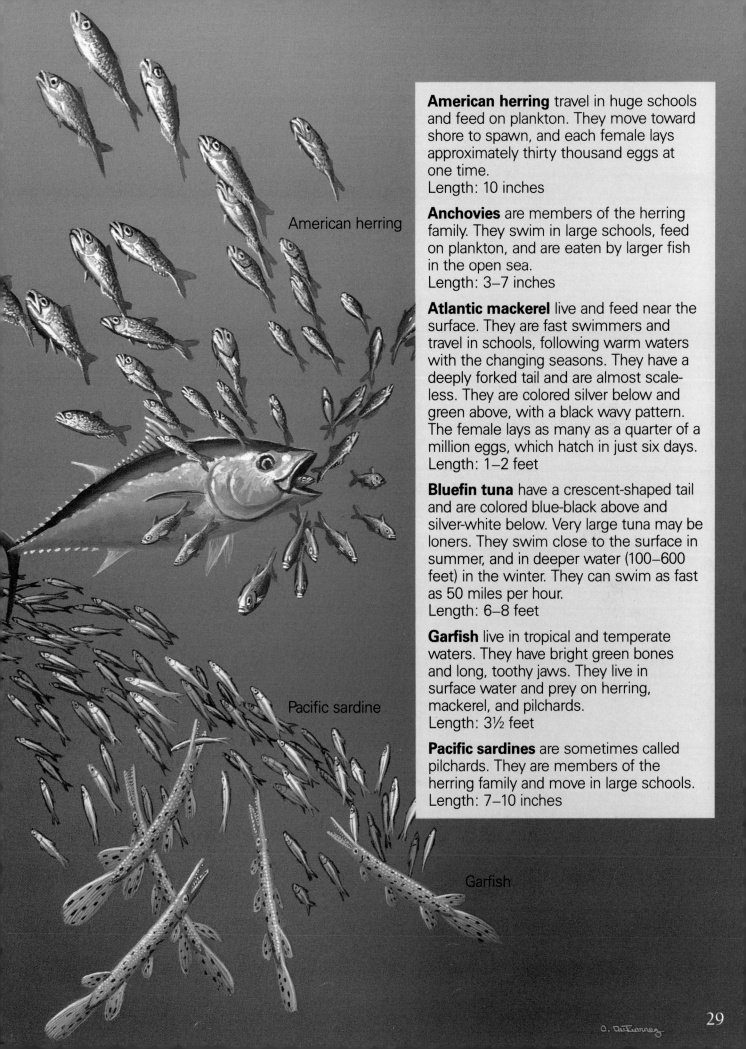

American herring travel in huge schools and feed on plankton. They move toward shore to spawn, and each female lays approximately thirty thousand eggs at one time.
Length: 10 inches

Anchovies are members of the herring family. They swim in large schools, feed on plankton, and are eaten by larger fish in the open sea.
Length: 3–7 inches

Atlantic mackerel live and feed near the surface. They are fast swimmers and travel in schools, following warm waters with the changing seasons. They have a deeply forked tail and are almost scale-less. They are colored silver below and green above, with a black wavy pattern. The female lays as many as a quarter of a million eggs, which hatch in just six days.
Length: 1–2 feet

Bluefin tuna have a crescent-shaped tail and are colored blue-black above and silver-white below. Very large tuna may be loners. They swim close to the surface in summer, and in deeper water (100–600 feet) in the winter. They can swim as fast as 50 miles per hour.
Length: 6–8 feet

Garfish live in tropical and temperate waters. They have bright green bones and long, toothy jaws. They live in surface water and prey on herring, mackerel, and pilchards.
Length: 3½ feet

Pacific sardines are sometimes called pilchards. They are members of the herring family and move in large schools.
Length: 7–10 inches

American herring

Pacific sardine

Garfish

THE DEEP SEA

Some of the strangest-looking fish live their entire lives in the dark, cold depths of the sea. Here, where the sun's rays can't reach, food is scarce. These fish are scavengers. They live on food that falls from the surface and midwaters. Yet these deep-sea dwellers are well adapted to the endless night. Many have luminous organs that blink on and off like flashing lights. These lights may be used to lure prey, attract mates, scare off predators, or keep a school of fish together.

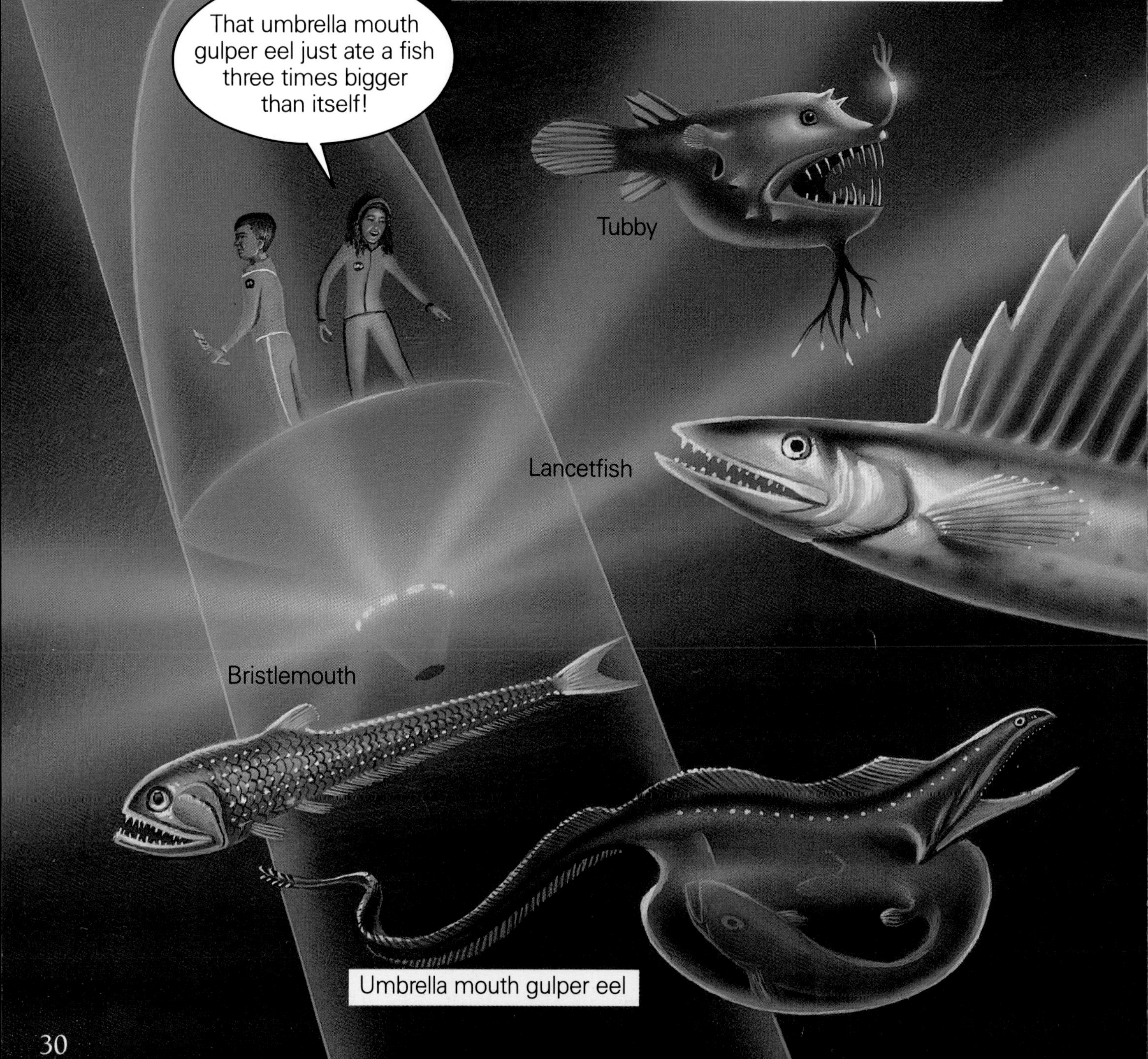

That umbrella mouth gulper eel just ate a fish three times bigger than itself!

Tubby

Lancetfish

Bristlemouth

Umbrella mouth gulper eel

Common blackdevil
deep-sea angler

Deep-sea angler

Lanternfish

Bristlemouth have light spots along the sides of their body. There are probably more of these small relatives of the herring than any other fish in the sea.
Length: 3 inches

Common blackdevil deep-sea anglers are totally parasitic. In order to reproduce, the male anglerfish spends most of its life attached to the female.
Length: 8 inches

Deep-sea anglers have a luminous lure on the end of their "fishing rod": this is used to attract smaller fish. Once prey is within reach, the angler opens its huge mouth.
Length: 3–4 inches

Lancetfish are one of the few large fish that feed on small deep-water fish. They have a high dorsal fin and fanglike teeth.
Length: 6 feet

Lanternfish have a luminous body. Males of the species can identify females by a luminous organ beneath the females' tail.
Length: 3 inches

Tubby are anglerfish with a weedlike chin barbel and a luminous lure.
Length: 3 inches

Umbrella mouth gulper eels have a big mouth and will eat whatever happens to drift by. They have tiny eyes on the front of their head and a red light on their tail that attracts fish.
Length: 2 feet

MORE FISH OF THE DEEP SEA

Most of these deep-sea fish are relatively small. Many have large eyes that are directed upward like binoculars. They may also have fanglike teeth and barbels under their chins.

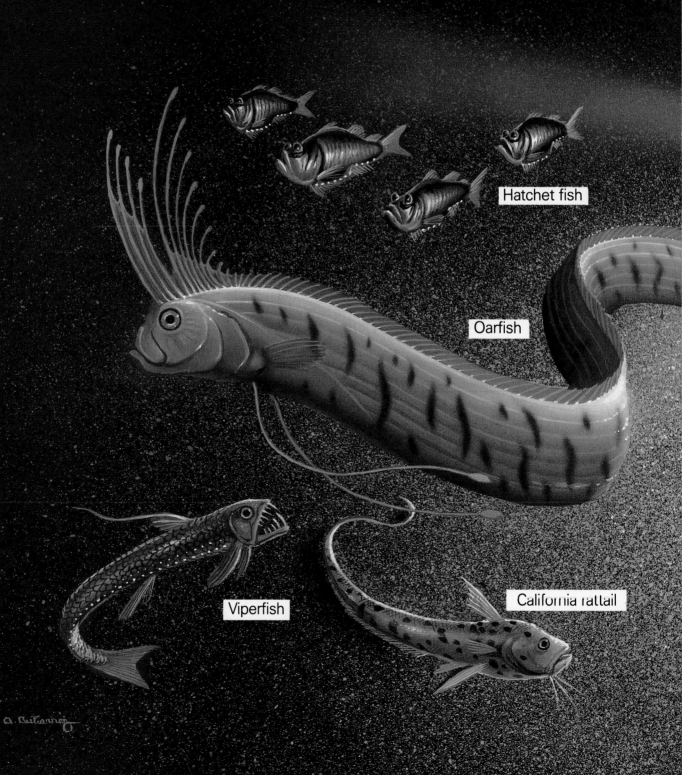

Hatchet fish

Oarfish

Viperfish

California rattail

SHARK TANK

We have now entered the shark tank. There are about three hundred known species of sharks. Some can be found in shallow coastal waters. Others live in the open sea. And still others live at depths of as much as 9,000 feet.

Here, in the shark tank, we can see the distant descendants of fish that lived in the seas 300 million years ago. Many species of animals have come and gone in that time, but sharks have changed very little over the ages.

Remora

Pilot fish

Tiger shark

Thresher shark

Sandbar sharks can be found from the tropics to New England. They eat bottom fish.
Length: 6½ feet

Tiger sharks may use as many as 24,000 triangular teeth over a ten-year period. They eat other sharks and rays, and are related to the blue shark.
Length: 10 feet and more

Thresher sharks are surface swimmers that hunt schools of herring and mackerel. They thrash their long tail back and forth in schools of small fish to stun or kill them and can gulp down a few hundred at a time.
Length: 20 feet

Fish That Follow Sharks

Pilot fish follow sharks and ships. They feed on tidbits big fish leave along the way.

Remora are two-foot-long hitchhikers. They attach themselves to sharks and other large fish by using the oval sucking disc on their head. They dine on the leftovers of their host.

Sandbar shark

SHARK TANK

By reputation, sharks are often thought of as ferocious killers. Yet, only about twelve of the roughly three hundred kinds of sharks are known to attack people.

Sharks are ideally designed to hunt their prey. Their torpedo-shaped bodies are sleek and muscular. They are covered with sharp, toothlike scales. Their jaws are lined with rows of razor-sharp teeth. When one tooth breaks or falls out, a tooth from the second row moves forward.

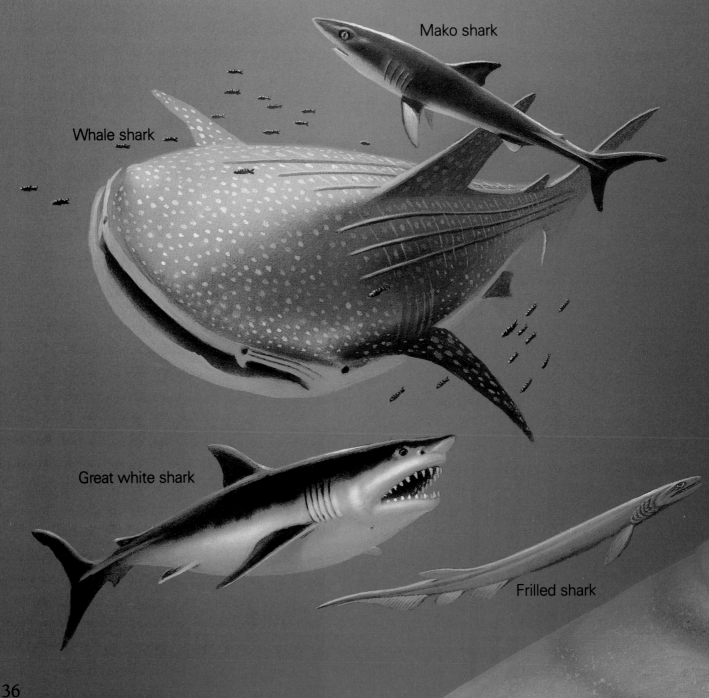

Mako shark

Whale shark

Great white shark

Frilled shark

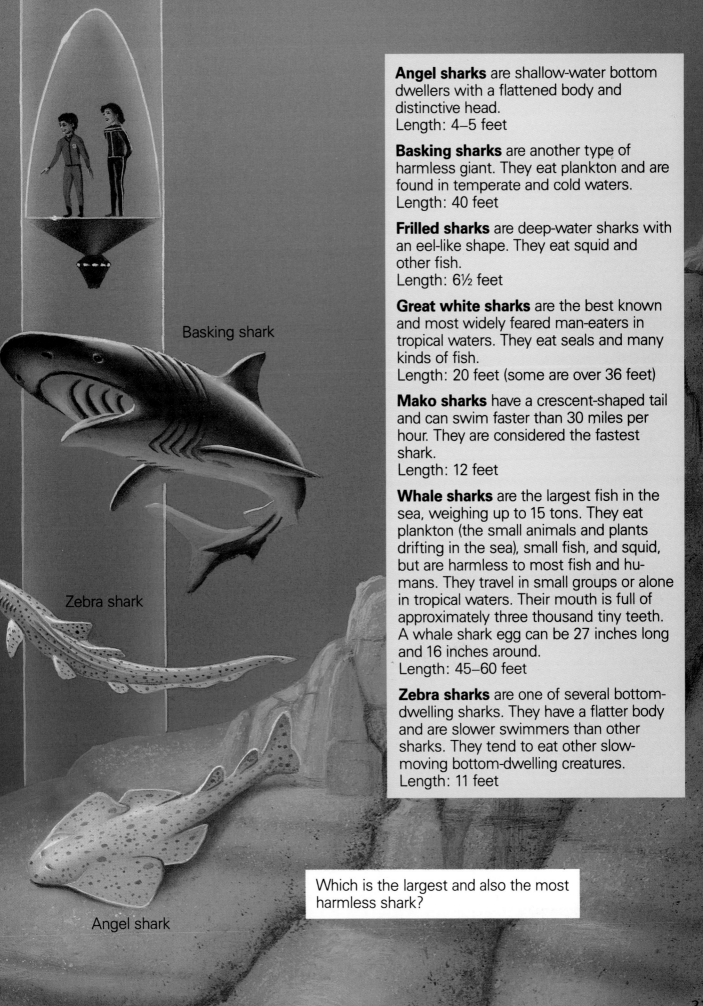

Basking shark

Zebra shark

Angel shark

Angel sharks are shallow-water bottom dwellers with a flattened body and distinctive head.
Length: 4–5 feet

Basking sharks are another type of harmless giant. They eat plankton and are found in temperate and cold waters.
Length: 40 feet

Frilled sharks are deep-water sharks with an eel-like shape. They eat squid and other fish.
Length: 6½ feet

Great white sharks are the best known and most widely feared man-eaters in tropical waters. They eat seals and many kinds of fish.
Length: 20 feet (some are over 36 feet)

Mako sharks have a crescent-shaped tail and can swim faster than 30 miles per hour. They are considered the fastest shark.
Length: 12 feet

Whale sharks are the largest fish in the sea, weighing up to 15 tons. They eat plankton (the small animals and plants drifting in the sea), small fish, and squid, but are harmless to most fish and humans. They travel in small groups or alone in tropical waters. Their mouth is full of approximately three thousand tiny teeth. A whale shark egg can be 27 inches long and 16 inches around.
Length: 45–60 feet

Zebra sharks are one of several bottom-dwelling sharks. They have a flatter body and are slower swimmers than other sharks. They tend to eat other slow-moving bottom-dwelling creatures.
Length: 11 feet

Which is the largest and also the most harmless shark?

ANATOMY OF A SHARK

Box Shark

Sharks have a very small brain but large olfactory organs for smelling. Their sense of smell is so keen that they can smell a drop of blood dissolved in a million drops of water. In fact, the smell of blood can set off a feeding frenzy. Sharks may become so aggressive that they end up eating not only their prey but each other.

Most sharks bear live and fully formed young, and many produce a brood of three or four. However, some, like the cat shark, lay eggs that hatch among the seaweed.

Sharks have skeletons made of cartilage—like the tip of your nose. Unlike other fish they have no gas bladder to keep them afloat. So, like perpetual motion machines, some sharks must constantly swim, or they will sink to the bottom.

The color of a shark is often a good clue as to where it lives. For example, the sandbar shark matches the sandy bottom where it dwells. The blue shark, which is blue above and silver-white below, blends with the open sea.

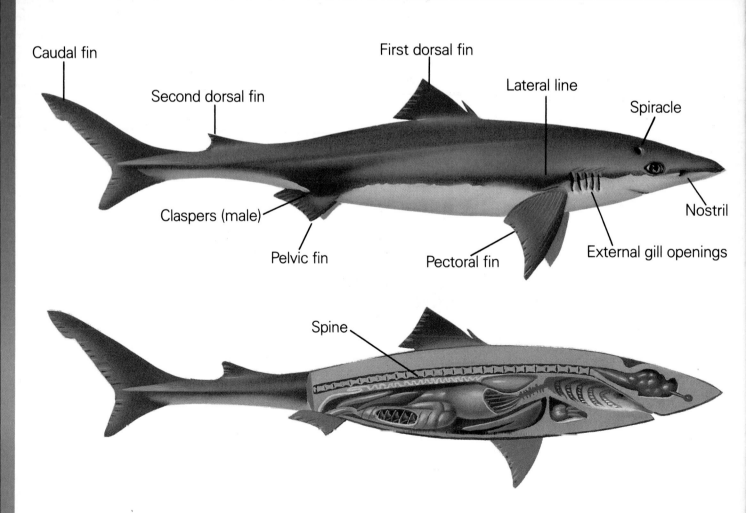

Caudal fin

Second dorsal fin

First dorsal fin

Lateral line

Spiracle

Nostril

Claspers (male)

Pelvic fin

Pectoral fin

External gill openings

Spine

A Cat Shark Egg
Most sharks are born live, but the cat shark's egg hatches from an egg case. The long tendrils on the egg case are designed to catch onto seaweed until the embryo hatches.

SKATES AND RAYS

Here, you can see just a few of the 400–500 species of skates and rays. Like their relatives the sharks, they have skeletons made of cartilage. With their flattened bodies and rippling, winglike fins, these fish seem to glide through the sea like giant bats.

Rays are usually larger than skates, with more rounded faces and are armed with barbed spines. Skates are smaller and quite harmless. Another difference is that rays give birth to live young while female skates lay eggs in cases.

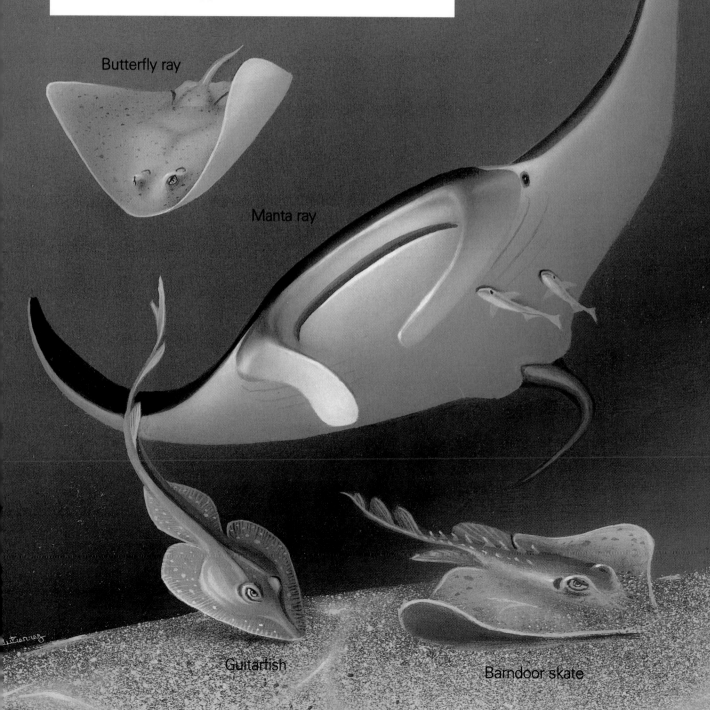

Butterfly ray

Manta ray

Guitarfish

Barndoor skate

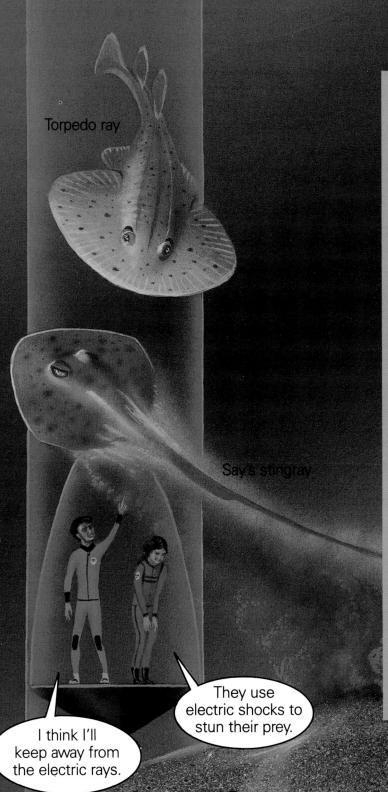

Torpedo ray

Say's stingray

Barndoor skates have a distinctive, pointed snout. They eat bottom fish and crabs.
Length: 5 feet

Butterfly rays have a short tail and wide, triangular wings.
Length: 6 feet wide

Guitarfish live in shallow tropical and temperate waters. They travel in schools and have blunt teeth for crushing mollusks.
Length: 5–6 feet

Manta rays, like whale sharks, are harmless giants that feed on shellfish and small animals in warm surface waters. Their devilish-looking "horns" create a funnel-like mouth for easy feeding. They leap above surface waters and return with a thunderous clap. This leaping may be one way to get free of lice.
Length: Up to 20 feet

Say's stingrays are diamond-shaped, with a whiplike tail that is longer than their body. The venomous spine on its tail can make painful wounds. They live in shallow, warm waters.
Length: 7 feet

Torpedo rays are one of thirty species of electric rays. They have an organ in their wings which can give an electric shock of 200 volts. They use electric shocks to stun their prey and to keep rivals away at breeding time.
Length: 3–5 feet

They use electric shocks to stun their prey.

I think I'll keep away from the electric rays.

Mermaid's Purses are the egg cases of skates. Young skates hatch from these leathery, horned cases. The egg is fertilized inside the female and then ejected into the sea. It takes 5–15 months for the young to develop. Rays are born live, like most sharks.

SEA MAMMALS
WHALES, DOLPHINS, AND PORPOISES

Some of the largest and most intelligent animals in the sea belong to the group of mammals known as cetaceans. They include whales, dolphins, and porpoises.

Like all mammals, cetaceans have lungs and must come to the surface for air. But all these creatures spend their entire lives in the water.

Even though they are fewer in number than fish or invertebrates, mammals are some of the most fascinating creatures in the sea. Like land mammals, sea mammals are warm-blooded. Their young are born live and suckled with milk. Sea mammals can dive to great depths but must come to the surface to fill their lungs with air.

Blue whale

Sperm whale

Killer whale

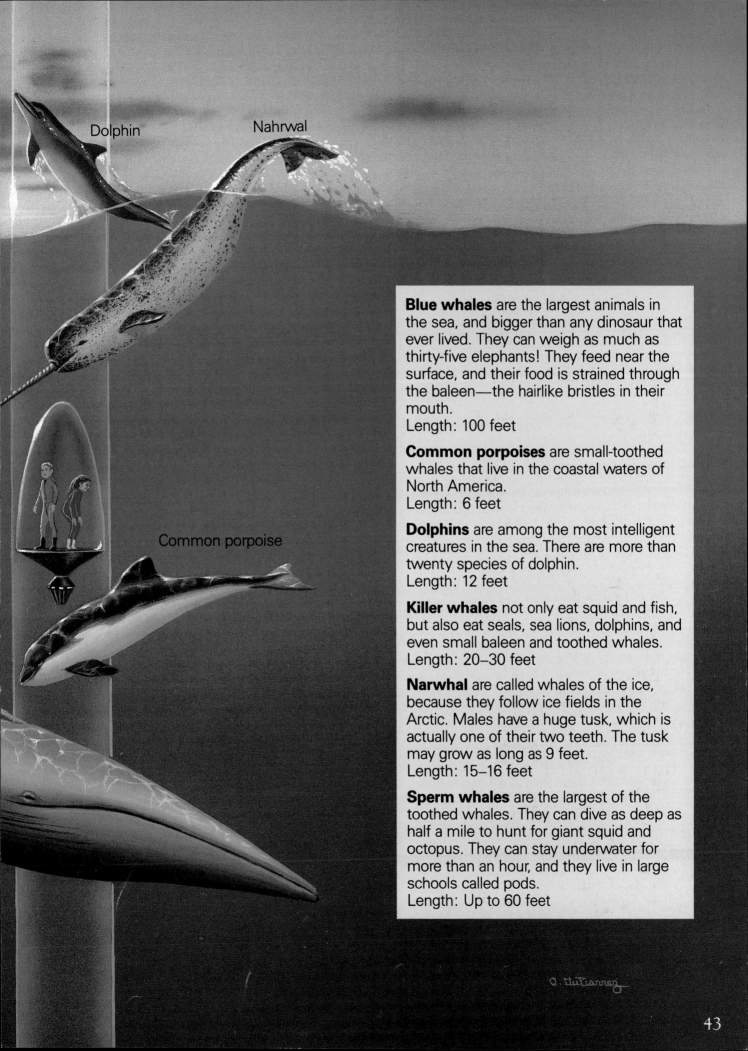

Dolphin

Nahrwal

Common porpoise

Blue whales are the largest animals in the sea, and bigger than any dinosaur that ever lived. They can weigh as much as thirty-five elephants! They feed near the surface, and their food is strained through the baleen—the hairlike bristles in their mouth.
Length: 100 feet

Common porpoises are small-toothed whales that live in the coastal waters of North America.
Length: 6 feet

Dolphins are among the most intelligent creatures in the sea. There are more than twenty species of dolphin.
Length: 12 feet

Killer whales not only eat squid and fish, but also eat seals, sea lions, dolphins, and even small baleen and toothed whales.
Length: 20–30 feet

Narwhal are called whales of the ice, because they follow ice fields in the Arctic. Males have a huge tusk, which is actually one of their two teeth. The tusk may grow as long as 9 feet.
Length: 15–16 feet

Sperm whales are the largest of the toothed whales. They can dive as deep as half a mile to hunt for giant squid and octopus. They can stay underwater for more than an hour, and they live in large schools called pods.
Length: Up to 60 feet

MORE SEA MAMMALS

Unlike the cetaceans, seals, sea lions, and sea otters spend some of their time on shore. They enter the water to feed, to escape predators, and sometimes to mate. Other sea mammals like the manatee and the dugong—both endangered species—never leave the water. They live in sheltered bays and lagoons, and stay close to land.

Alaska or Northern fur seal

California sea lion

Manatee

Dugong

Walrus

O. Dikienna

al

Sea otter

Alaska or Northern fur seals have thick hind flippers for walking and thick underfur for warmth. They can swim as fast as 17 miles per hour and dive as deep as 240 feet. They travel alone or in small herds.
Length: Females to 5 feet
       Males to 7 feet

California sea lions are playful creatures that are rarely found farther than 10 miles from shore. They have thick hind flippers that can turn forward so they can walk on land. They make honking, barking sounds. They are found off the Pacific coast as far north as British Columbia. They live in herds.
Length: Females to 6 feet
       Males to 8 feet

Dugongs live in pairs or small family groups. They are found in the Red Sea along the east African coast, in the Bay of Bengal, along the coastal areas of Indonesia and northern Australia. They have short flippers and a sickle-shaped tail. They eat plants in shallow water.
Length: 8–10 feet

Harbor seals have flippers that cannot turn forward, so they have to wriggle on land rather than walk. They can stay underwater for as long as 20 minutes. They swim up to 15 miles per hour. They live in pairs on the shoreline along coastal waters and often mate for life.
Length: Up to 6 feet

Manatees are also called sea cows. They are sluggish, square-snouted creatures with a broad head and thick upper lip. They are plant eaters and live in small groups in lagoons and brackish waters along the Atlantic coast of the United States from North Carolina southward to the Caribbean.
Length: 7–13 feet

Sea otters live just beyond the shore in kelp beds and can dive to depths of up to 60 feet. They are the only sea mammal that have no fatty blubber under their hide. They have webbed hind feet and a large head with small, pointed ears.
Length: Up to 5 feet

Walrus live in remote areas off Greenland and the Arctic in herds of one hundred or more. They have a thick body with tough, wrinkled skin and a 3-inch layer of blubber. They also have ivory tusks, which can grow up to 3½ feet long. They swim at 10–12 miles per hour and make bellowing and trumpeting sounds.
Length: Females 10–12 feet
       Males 8–10 feet

From the Florida Keys to Australia's Great Barrier Reef, coral reefs are being choked to death by dirty sewage and other pollutants that block the sunlight and can kill the entire ecosystem.

In 1954, fishing boats caught 21.6 million tons of fish.
In 1983, they caught three times as much.
In 1991, they caught over 100 million tons!
How can we stop this overfishing?

Drift nets 40 miles long catch more than fish. Scientists estimate that 200,000 mammals such as sea lions, whales, seals, birds, and porpoises are trapped and killed annually by nets.

Plastic trash turns up on the most remote beaches in the world. It doesn't just litter—it kills birds, turtles, whales, and sea creatures that get caught in it or swallow it.

SAVE OUR SEAS

This concludes our tour through the Oceanarium. You've seen that the ocean is a vast and beautiful place, but as this hall shows our oceans are in great danger. Every day millions of gallons of chemical wastes, fertilizers, untreated sewage, and other pollutants run off into rivers and get carried out to sea. The polluted waters carry disease and destruction to both humans and sea creatures. Some commercial fishing boats even dump cyanide poison into the ocean to stun fish. As the waters become dirty and poisoned, so does the food chain—from microscopic plankton to the fish we eat.

But it's not just pollution that is killing fish. Huge fishing boats and drift nets are scooping up fish faster than they can reproduce. If these practices continue, there just might come a day when the only place you can see such underwater splendor is at the Oceanarium.

Index

A
Alaska (or Northern) fur
    seal, 45
Anchovy, 29
Angel shark, 11, 37
Atlantic wolffish, 15

B
Barndoor skate, 41
Barracuda, 19
Barreleye, 33
Basking shark, 37
Blenny, 13
Blue marlin, 25
Blue whale, 43
Bonefish, 15
Box shark, 38
Bristlemouth, 31
Butterfish, 17
Butterfly ray, 41

C
California rattail, 10, 33
California sea lion, 45
Catfish, 14–15
Cat shark, 39
Cetacean, 42–43, 44
Cleaner wrasse, 21
Clown butterfly fish, 19
Clown fish, 19
Cod, 10, 15, 23, 33
Common jack, 17
Common porpoise, 42–43,
    47
Coral, 18–21, 46
Crab, 12, 15, 23, 41
Crustacean, 15, 17

D
Deep-sea angler, 11, 31
Dolphin, 42–43

Dolphin fish, 25
Dugong, 44–45

E
Ecosystem, 46–47

F
Flounder, 12–13, 22–23
Flying fish, 10, 24–25
Frilled shark, 37

G
Garfish, 11, 29
Great white shark, 37
Guitarfish, 41

H
Haddock, 9, 11, 17, 23, 33
Hake, 10, 33
Halibut, 11, 23
Harbor seal, 45
Hatchet fish, 33
Herring, 7, 17, 23, 25, 26,
    29, 31, 35

J
Jellyfish, 12, 25

K
Kelpfish, 13
Killer whale, 43

L
Lancetfish, 31
Lanternfish, 10, 31
Lionfish, 21
Longhorn sculpin, 13
Lumpfish, 13

M
Mackerel, 17, 25, 29, 35
Mako shark, 37

Mammal, 9, 42–45, 47
Manatee (or sea cow), 45
Manta ray, 10, 41
Menhaden, 15, 25
Mermaid's purse, 41
Mojarra, 15
Mollusk, 15, 19, 25, 41
Moray eel, 21

N
Narwhal, 43
Nassau grouper, 21
Needlefish, 17
North American striped
    bass, 17

O
Oarfish, 11, 33
Ocean sunfish, 10, 25
Ocean triggerfish, 21
Octopus, 14–15, 19

P
Pacific sardine, 29
Parrot fish, 19
Pigfish, 17
Pilot fish, 35
Pipefish, 13
Plaice, 10, 23
Plankton, 19, 29, 37, 47
Pollution, 46–47
Porcupine fish, 13

Q
Queen angelfish, 21

R
Remora, 35

S
Sailfish, 25

Sandbar shark, 35
Say's stingray, 41
School, 15, 17, 24–25, 26–
    27, 28–29, 35, 41, 43
Sea horse, 7, 13
Sea otter, 44–45
Sergeant-major, 19
Shanny, 13
Shellfish, 15, 17, 23, 41
Shrimp, 12, 15, 21, 23
Snipe eel, 10
Sole, 23
Sperm whale, 43
Spotted goatfish, 19
Squid, 15, 25, 37, 43
Stonefish, 21
Swordfish, 25

T
Tarpon, 15
Thresher shark, 35
Tiger shark, 35
Torpedo ray, 41
Tripletail, 17
Tripodfish, 10, 33
Tubby, 31
Tuna 8, 10, 26, 29

V
Viperfish, 33

W
Walrus, 45
Whale shark, 37

Y
Yellowtail snapper, 26–27

Z
Zebra shark, 37

About the Contributors

Joanne Oppenheim, the author, has written more than thirty books for and about children. She is senior editor in the Publications Division of the Bank Street College for Education in New York. A former elementary school teacher, she is the author of the Mrs. Peloki series, which was listed several times among the IRA Children's Choices. She also wrote *Have You Seen Birds?* which was selected as an outstanding Science Book by the National Science Teachers Association and the Children's Book Council and which also won the Canadian Children's Council Literature Prize.

Alan Gutierrez, the illustrator, graduated from the Art Center College of Design in 1982. He has illustrated several children's books, including the *Prince of Whales, Space Swimmers,* and *Space Winners.* His realistic style has been sought for over 150 covers for paperback books, periodicals, and game and toy box sets. He has won many awards for his art, including the DESI Award for editorial illustration in 1987 and received a Certificate of Merit from New York Society of

Illustrators. He lives in Arizona with his wife and three-year-old daughter, Rachel.

Ellie Fries and Merryl Kafka, the science consultants, are the Director and Assistant Director of Education at the N.Y. Aquarium. Receiving a B.S. degree from Cornell University, Ms. Fries joined the N.Y. Aquarium as an instructor in 1978 where she specialized in program and curriculum development. She has been responsible for creating and implementing children and family workshops and holiday programs. Ms. Kafka received her masters degree in biology from New York University and is presently pursuing a doctoral degree in Instructional Leadership at St. John's University. She has been an educational consultant with Bank Street College of Education, the American Museum of Natural History, and the New York City Board of Education. They are both members of the executive board of the New York State Marine Education Association where they have received several awards for outstanding contributions to marine science education.